STARS IN MY EYES

A Little Something Extra
ICE CREAM

written by:
Michelle Norwood

inspired by:
Hunter Norwood

illustrated by:
Ashton Smith

Published and printed in the United States of America.

First Edition
Norwood, Michelle
Stars In My Eyes / Michelle Norwood
Originally published: 2020, AL

Layout Design by Mike Dozier,
www.MKADesigns.com

Printing by Ingram Spark,
Lavergne, TN

Dedication

This book is dedicated to our amazing children who are the shining stars in my life! Hope, Tori, Hunter, and Brodie; you've each put a star in my eye that shines brighter with every thought of you.

To every family we have met through the journey of Down syndrome, thank you! Our world is brighter because of our friendships and our tribe.

To my husband, Anthony, our parents and siblings; thank you for believing in me and always supporting my passion for advocacy, opportunity, and purpose!

And finally to Hunter! Thank you for rockin' those designer genes! You are an amazing human and your life makes me want to be better!

I have stars in my eyes.

Since the day I was born, my parents noticed stars in my eyes!

Mom says she gazed into my eyes for hours, looking at the stars and wondering why they were there.

But, deep down, my mom always knew.

The doctor told my mom
the stars are called
Brushfield Spots
and are one of the
common characteristics
of Down syndrome.

My mom says I have stars in my eyes to remind the world that I have hopes and dreams. She says the stars are common in the eyes of people with *Down syndrome* because we were made to shine, just like the stars in the sky.

When I was a toddler, I wanted to walk. I had to try harder and work longer than other toddlers. But, the stars in my eyes reminded my family that the day would come when I could walk.

And the day DID come! And we celebrated! And I have never slowed down!

When I was a little boy, I wanted to play sports. Even though things did not come as easy for me as other children, the stars in my eyes reminded my community to keep helping me reach my dream. With extra help from my family, coaches, and teammates, I have been able to hit homeruns, score points in basketball, and even run a touchdown.

The stars in my eyes keep
showing the world
that I'm a
BIG DEAL!

When I was a teenager, I told my parents I wanted to have a job someday. Every night, my mom looked into the stars in my eyes and told me I could be anything I wanted to be.

These stars in my eyes are great reminders of that!

One day, my parents helped me start my own business. An ice cream truck business.

Now, I get to go places every day, selling ice cream and making people smile.

My friends help me work in the ice cream truck.

They have stars in their eyes too! When we work together, we shine like a constellation.

We travel around in the ice cream truck reminding the world that we have stars in our eyes for a reason.

We have potential!

We have a purpose!

My name is Hunter and I want
to remind you to always look for
the stars in others' eyes. The
stars are great reminders that
everyone's possibilities are
OUT OF THIS WORLD!

He counts the stars and
knows each of them
by name.
Psalm 147:4

The One who put the
stars in the sky, put
the stars in my eyes;
how could I not be
awesome?

Brushfield spots are light-colored condensations of the surface of the mid-iris in the human eye, often seen in people who have Down syndrome. ("Brushfield Spots." Stedman's Medical Dictionary for the Health Professions and Nursing. 5th ed. 2005. Print.)

Brushfield spots are named after the physician, Thomas Brushfield, who first described them in his medical thesis in 1924.

(https://www.medicinenet.com/script/main/art.asp?articlekey=6570)

Brushfield spots occur in a large percentage of people who have Down syndrome, but can also occur in the eyes of people who do not.

(https://en.wikipedia.org/wiki/Brushfield_spots)

Regardless of whether or not the "stars" are visible in a person's eyes, always remember that every person is born with the ability to light up the world and do great things!

Illustrator, Ashton Smith, teamed up with some of our Ice Cream Experts, who also happen to have stars in their eyes. Together, they created their own beautiful "starry" masterpieces. Each are displayed on the following pages.

Artist: **Andrew**

Andrew enjoys Southern gospel music, being with friends and helping around his house. He loves to pray for others and to work in the ice cream truck.

Artist: **Blake**

Blake is very funny, kind, sensitive, and honest. He enjoys swimming, music, family game night, board and video games. Blake loves working in the ice cream truck and wants to be a famous YouTuber some day.

Artist: **Braxton**

Braxton enjoys riding his bicycle, swimming, playing basketball and baseball, watching movies and listening to music. He loves spending time with family and friends and working in the ice cream truck.

Artist: **Hunter**

Hunter enjoys fishing, hunting and playing all sports. He loves to go to the beach, spend time with his family, study the weather, and of course, work in the ice cream truck with his friends.

Artist: **Jada**

Jada enjoys all things Disney and is a social media queen. She loves to play basketball, softball and to work with her friends in the ice cream truck.

Artist: **Jaelynn**

Jaelynn enjoys camping, singing in church, pretending to be a teacher and reading to her baby dolls. She loves being with her family and little sister and showing off the picture of herself that is on the side of Hunter's ice cream truck.

Artist: **Kendle**

Kendle enjoys swimming, singing, cooking, and swinging outside. She loves dreaming of her future, trying new things, having quiet time and working in the ice cram truck. Her favorite color is rainbow sparkle.

Artist: **Libby**

Libby enjoys shopping, dressing up, eating at nice restaurants and going to the movies. Libby loves all things pink, spending time with her friends and family, and working in the ice cream truck.

Artist: **Rusty**

Rusty enjoys organizing his room, dancing, playing baseball, basketball and bowling. He loves to spend time with his friends and family and to work in the ice cream truck.

Artist: **Ryan**

Ryan enjoys attending church, singing in the choir, teaching children's church, reading the Bible and playing the guitar. He loves spending time with friends and family, working at Lowe's in the lawn and garden department, as well as, in the ice cream truck.

If you'd like to learn more about the wonderment of Down syndrome, check out the following resources:

National Down Syndrome Congress
www.ndsccenter.org

National Down Syndrome Society
www.ndss.org

Down Syndrome Resource Foundation
www.nads.org

Global Down Syndrome Foundation
www.globaldownsyndrome.org

Full Life Ahead
www.fulllifeahead.org

Pregnancy Centers/Life Affirming Choices/Adundant Life
www.care-net.org

Heartbeat International
www.heartbeatinternational.org

Pre-Born
www.preborn.org

CPSIA information can be obtained
at www.ICGtesting.com
Printed in the USA
BVHW021858160820
PP11083500001B/4

9 781087 901855